P9-COP-209

Nelly Gnu and Daddy Too

Anna Dewdney

VIKING
An Imprint of Penguin Group (USA)

This book is dedicated to my father, George Luhrmann.
With special thanks to Tracy and Denise.

VIKING
Published by the Penguin Group / Penguin Group (USA) LLC / 375 Hudson Street / New York, New York 10014

USA / Canada / UK / Ireland / Australia / New Zealand / India / South Africa / China

penguin.com
A Penguin Random House Company

First published in the United States of America by Viking, an imprint of Penguin Young Readers Group, 2014

Copyright © 2014 by Anna Dewdney

Penguin supports copyright. Copyright fuels creativity, encourages diverse voices, promotes free speech, and creates a vibrant culture. Thank you
for buying an authorized edition of this book and for complying with copyright laws by not reproducing, scanning, or distributing any part of it
in any form without permission. You are supporting writers and allowing Penguin to continue to publish books for every reader.

LIBRARY OF CONGRESS CATALOGING-IN-PUBLICATION DATA
Dewdney, Anna.
Nelly Gnu and Daddy too / by Anna Dewdney.
pages cm
Summary: Nelly Gnu spends a day building a playhouse with her father.
ISBN 978-0-670-01227-5 (hardcover)
[1. Stories in rhyme. 2. Fathers and daughters—Fiction. 3. Playhouses—Fiction. 4. Gnus—Fiction.] I. Title.
PZ8.3.D498Nel 2014   [E]—dc23   2013032619

Manufactured in China   Designed by Kate Renner

10 9 8 7 6 5 4 3 2 1

Nelly loves her Daddy Gnu.

He always knows
just what to do.

A great big box, some tape,
and string—
Daddy can make anything!

First they measure.

Then they draw.

Nelly tapes,

and Daddy saws.

And then, they add a little glue.
Nelly and her Daddy Gnu!

A perfect little house for one!

But Nelly thinks it's not quite done. . . .

It needs some flowers, just a few.

Time to shop
with Daddy Gnu.

A big adventure
to the store!

Plants and hammers,
ladders, more.

Would she like a better view?

Take a ride
on Daddy Gnu!

More colors than she's ever seen—
purple, yellow, pink, and green!

Nelly finds the
perfect blue.

Daddy gets some brushes, too.

Out with Daddy—
hip hooray!
It's a super-duper day
for Nelly and her Daddy Gnu. . . .

Uh-oh!

Swooping, zooming,
way up high!

Daddy holds her,
and she flies!

Guess who loves his Nelly? Who?
Yes, it's Daddy—Daddy Gnu.

Time for checkout at the store.
Daddy adds just *one* thing more.

A special day for just these two—
Nelly and her Daddy Gnu.

Paint the house with brick designs.
Big bright flowers,
climbing vines.

There's nothing that these two can't do—
Nelly and her Daddy Gnu.

Time for dinner.
Daddy cooks.

Then they read their
favorite books.

Every night and every day,
Daddy makes it all OK.
He always knows just what to do . . .

Nelly's Daddy, Daddy Gnu.